RAIN DANCE

by Kathi Appelt
pictures by Emilie Chollat

HarperFestival®
A Division of HarperCollinsPublishers

Water drops

1

Froggie hops

Spiders skitter

3 Chickies flitter

4

Calves swish

5

Piggies squish

Rabbits hurry

Ducklings scurry

8 Puppies splatter

Kittens scatter

10 Ponies prance